The Healed Frog

By Julia Pelon

The
Healed
Frog

First Printing, 2020

ISBN

979-8-64253-285-0

Dedication:

To my family in New York.
I love you.

Ernie is a green frog
who lives on a great big lake.

Every day, when Ernie wakes up,
he is so happy. He knows God
has blessed him with a
beautiful place to live,

plenty of food to eat,

and special friends to play with.

He thanks God each day
for all that He has given
him.

One day, after Ernie finished playing
with two of his friends, he decided
to head home.

As he was hopping through the tall grass,
something happened.

"Ouch!" Ernie said. "That hurts."
He looked down and saw
a scratch on the back of
his right leg. "It must have
happened when I hopped
past that sharp rock,"
he thought. "Well, I'm sure
it'll be just fine tomorrow."

When Ernie woke up the next day,
his leg hurt more than ever.
"Oh no! I should have taken better
care of my leg," he said.

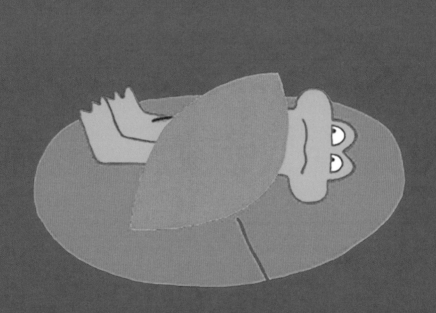

He wondered what he should
do to help it get better.
"I'll go talk to some
of my friends for advice."

So off he went. Ernie ran into
Mr. Robin. "Mr. Robin, can you help me?
I have a scratch on my leg. What
shall I do so it will heal?" he asked.
"Put your leg in cool water for a while
to clean it," said Mr. Robin.

"Okay, thanks!" said Ernie
and he quickly hopped over
to the lake and jumped in.
"Hmm... my leg feels cooler
but it still hurts," thought
Ernie. "I better go see
"Mr. Butterfly."

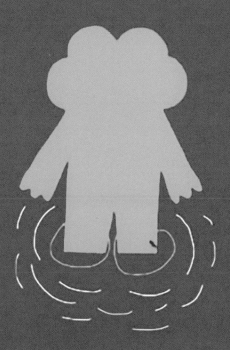

"Mr. Butterfly, can you help me?
I have a scratch on my leg.
I put it in water to clean it, but
what else do I need to do so
it will heal?" Ernie asked.

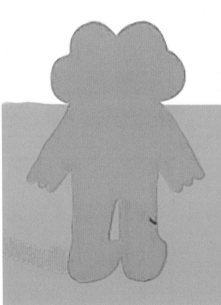

"You need some medicine to put on it,
said Mr. Butterfly. "Find some herbs
and rub it on the scratch."
"Okay, thanks," said Ernie, and
off he went.

He found some herbs and put it on the
scratch. "Wow! It is feeling better,
but I wonder if there is something
else I need to do," thought Ernie.
"I better go see Mr. Owl."

When Ernie turned around, he saw Mr. Owl up in a tree. "Mr. Owl, can you help me? I have a scratch on my leg.

I put it in water to clean it and rubbed some herbs on the scratch, but what else do I need to do so it will heal?" "Did you pray?" asked Mr. Owl. Ernie looked down for a moment then said in a low voice, "No, I didn't." So Mr. Owl responded, "God is a good God. It is His will that all of your needs are met, including healing."

Ernie prayed right there and thanked
God for healing his leg, and to
forgive him for not turning to Him first
for advice. He thanked Mr. Owl
and went home.

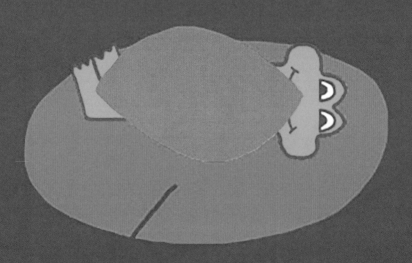

As Ernie laid in bed that night,
he was so happy knowing that
God loved him and was always
there to take care of him.

Ernie's leg quickly healed that week. When he saw his friends, he excitedly told them what God did for him as he prayed and asked Him for advice.

THE
END

For I will restore health to you
and heal you of your wounds.

Jeremiah 30:17

Fun Ideas and Activities to Compliment

The Healed Frog

I'm a teacher also, so I LOVE children, I LOVE books, I LOVE activities, and I LOVE fun! I decided to add some things that you can read or do with children that would make this amazing book even more fun. Enjoy!

List of Contents

Science and Math

1. What is a cut?
2. What is an infection?
3. What are germs?
4. Study ways to treat cuts naturally
5. Discuss bad ways to treat a cut
6. Herb study: study, research, grow
7. First Aid: strategies for treating cuts, scratches, etc.
8. Make First Aid Kits
9. Band-Aids: count, sort, identify types and purposes
10. Skin study of humans
11. Skin study of frogs
12. Discuss frog's anatomy and circulatory system
13. Discuss how the human body scabs and heals
14. Study human circulatory system

Art

1. On a piece of construction paper with an outline of a large cross on it, have children stick band-aids on it- "Jesus suffered for our healing"

2. Glue a picture of Jesus on construction paper; have children cut out pictures of people from advertisements, etc., to glue on paper with Jesus- "Jesus is our Healer"

3. Dirt/soil: hands on play- children play with scoops, etc.; discuss ways to thoroughly clean hands

4. Soapy water: play and then make bubble prints on paper

5. Hand print painting

6. Finger printing with ink pads

7. Before and after prayer Paper activity: Fold paper in half; children draw themselves on left and right side; left side sad with scratch, right side happy and healed

Music and Movement

1. Sing: "Head, shoulders, knees , and toes"
2. Sing: "The Blood of Jesus"
3. Act out helping to minister first aid
4. Provide opportunities for children to pray for others and speak healing scriptures
5. Act out doctor, nurse, paramedic
6. Play freeze tag

Character Building

1. Jesus is our Healer: discuss He always will and wants to heal each of us
2. Discuss we are His instruments to bring healing to others in His name; look for opportunities to pray for others
3. Importance of speaking God's word vs. constantly speaking of symptoms
4. Discuss authority we need to walk in over sickness and disease
5. Importance of going to God for healing and seeking His pathway for our healing
6. Discuss humility, patience, obedience concerning God's direction for healing
7. Discuss how God is not a respecter of persons

Stories from the Bible

1. Good Samaritan: Luke 10: 30-37
2. Blind man with mud: John 9: 1-11
3. Naaman: 2 Kings 5: 1-14
4. Jairus's daughter: Luke 8: 41-56
5. Woman with the issue of blood: Mark 5: 25-34
6. Servant of centurion healed: Luke 7: 2-10
7. Only son alive again: Luke 7: 11-15
8. Lame man healed: Acts 3: 1-11

Healing Scriptures

Isaiah 53: 5

But He was wounded for our transgressions,
He was bruised for our iniquities;

The chastisement for our peace was upon
Him,

And by His stripes we are healed.

Psalm 103: 3

Who forgives all your iniquities, Who heals
all your diseases,

1 Peter 2: 24

Who Himself bore our sins in His own body
on the tree, that we, having died to sins,
might live for righteousness- by whose
stripes you were healed.

Matthew 4: 24

Then His fame went throughout all Syria;
and they brought to Him all sick people who
were afflicted with various diseases and
torments, and those who were demon-
possessed, epileptics, and paralytics; and He
healed them.

3 John 2

Beloved, I pray that you may prosper in all things and be in health, just as your soul prospers.

Psalm 6: 2

Have mercy on me, O Lord, for I am weak;

O Lord, heal me, for my bones are troubled.

Psalm 30: 2

O Lord my God, I cried out to You, and You healed me.

Psalm 34: 19

Many are the afflictions of the righteous,

but the Lord delivers him out of them all.

Psalm 50: 15

Call upon Me in the day of trouble;

I will deliver you, and you shall glorify Me.

Psalm 107: 20

He sent His word and healed them,

and delivered them from their destructions.

Jeremiah 17: 14

Heal me, O Lord, and I shall be healed; save
me, and I shall be saved,

for You are my praise.

* New King James Version

Made in the USA
Columbia, SC
10 June 2022

61520719R00020